Chapter 1

IT WAS TIME to get up and Nick Butler's alarm clock was bleeping madly. 'Shut up!' he yelled and stuffed his head under the pillows. Obediently, the bright yellow clock fell silent. It was the very latest thing in alarms, the mere sound of your voice could stop it. But the lovely silence only lasted two minutes. Then it started bleeping again. To shut it up for good you had to press the black button on top. Nick would have to get out of bed and cross the room to his bookshelf where Mum had sneakily put it the night before. He was hopeless at getting up.

'Drop dead!' he bellowed when the clock started off again. He was warm and snug and in the middle of a terrific dream. He and Dad were out in mid-Atlantic and a great storm was blowing. He'd rather get on with his dream than go to school. It was Double Maths first lesson with horrible Miss Huggett, definitely a day for having one of his illnesses.

'Nick!' his mother yelled irritably

A SUPERCHAMP BOOK

MINTLAW PRIMARY

ANN   PILLING

THE BOY WITH
HIS LEG IN THE AIR

Illustrated by
Pauline King

HEINEMANN · LONDON

MINTLAW PRIMARY

for Ben, who was told to hop
A.P.

for John and Stewart,
with love and thanks
P.K.

William Heinemann Ltd
Michelin House, 81 Fulham Road
London SW3 6RB

LONDON   MELBOURNE   AUCKLAND

First published in 1991
Text © 1991 Ann Pilling
Illustrations © 1991 Pauline King
The right of Ann Pilling to be identified as author of this work has
been asserted by her in accordance with the Copyright, Designs and
Patents Act 1988

ISBN 0 434 97664 4
Produced by Mandarin Offset
Printed and bound in Hong Kong

A school pack of SUPERCHAMPS 13–18
is available from
Heinemann Educational Books
ISBN 0 435 00092 6

from the bedroom underneath. 'It's time you got up. Now come *on* . . . '

'*OK!*' and he flung aside the bedclothes. She was obviously in one of her moods. Baby Ellie had kept her up half the night, cutting another tooth.

'*Ow!*' It was very odd, but the minute he got to his feet a peculiar pain shot straight up his right leg. He sat down again, gave it a good rub, then tried standing on it, rather gingerly.

'*Ouch*!' There it was again, a truly awful pain that reached right up into his thigh, squeezing at his flesh like a pair of giant pincers. He'd never had such a pain in his life. It was horrific.

He sat down again on his bed, rolled up both pyjama legs and examined himself very carefully. His feet and ankles looked perfectly normal, so did his knees. So he gave his right leg another rub, stretched it, shook it, and wiggled his toes. Then he stood up and tried to walk across the room to switch his clock off.

'Aarghh . . . ' It was agony now. He'd only taken three steps and he'd collapsed on the floor. 'Mum,' he screamed, '*Mum*!'

'Oh, stop fooling around,' she shouted up the stairs. 'Ellie's being a real pain this morning, I could do without your antics . . . '

'But Mum, I can't *walk*.'

'Well, hop, then. Listen, I've no time for playing games this morning. If you're not down these stairs in five minutes there'll be *no breakfast*!'

For a minute Nick just sat there in a heap. There was no pain now, he felt perfectly well. His right leg only hurt if he put his weight on it. 'Mum!' he shouted, trying to sound as pathetic as possible, 'please come up, *please* . . . '

'SWITCH THAT ALARM OFF!' she shouted back, really angry now. 'I'm taking Ellie downstairs.'

So in desperation Nick crawled across the carpet, reached up for his clock and chucked it through the door. There was a crash and a tinkle, then Ellie started bawling. 'Oh heck,' he thought. 'What if it's hit her?' He was really quite fond of his little sister.

Up came his mother, bounding into the attic with the baby stuffed under her arm like a parcel. Nick wrinkled his nose. She most definitely needed changing. 'Ellie smellie,' she gurgled at him.

But Nick wasn't in gurgling mood. 'Every time I try to walk I get this *pain*,' he explained to his mother. 'It's agony. You'll have to phone Dr Simms.'

Mrs Butler looked at him suspiciously. She knew all about Nick's 'illnesses'. 'Walk towards me,' she said, and she watched him. But after just two steps he collapsed against her with a groan. 'It's no good, Mum, I must have done something to it. It's when I stand up that it hurts.'

'Hmm . . . ' she muttered, looking rather worried now. 'Perhaps you've

just sprained it, or something . . . I know, perhaps it's cramp. That's it, I bet it's cramp.'

'No,' Nick said miserably. 'I've tried rubbing it and everything. Nothing seems to do any good.' Now he couldn't walk he actually rather wanted to go to school, even if it was Miss Huggett.

What on earth was wrong with his leg?

Mum had to put his clothes on and carry him all the way downstairs. At the breakfast table she propped his 'bad' leg up on an upside down bucket. Then she went to phone the doctor.

When she came back she'd already got her coat on. '*Right*,' she said, 'we're off.'

'Off where?'

'Hospital.' And she draped his anorak

round his shoulders. 'Come on.'

'But *Mum* . . . can't we just ask Dr Simms for some tablets or something?' He didn't fancy hospital at all. Hospitals were full of strange smells and strange noises, and of brisk smiling nurses that wheeled you away and did funny things to you with needles and tweezers. He'd had enough of hospital the last time, when he was five, and he'd got a bus ticket stuck up his nose.

'Listen, Dr Simms says hospital's the best place. They've got all the special equipment there. He says they might have to take some X-rays so we're going straight to Out Patients. Now then, you've got to keep that leg *stiff*.'

'Have you rung for a taxi?' For something special Mrs Butler always used Lux-Lux Kabs in the High Street, and Nick rather fancied a taxi ride.

'Certainly not. It's rush hour and we'd get stuck in the traffic. No, you can go in this.'

Nick watched in horror as she wheeled Ellie's pram through from the hall. 'But *Mum* . . .' he began.

'Oh, stop fussing.' She dumped him in sideways, tucking Ellie in behind.

Off they went down the road with Nick's left leg dangling down and his right leg stuck straight out, across the pavement.

'Excuse *me* . . .' a woman said, dodging out of the way as the loaded pram bore down upon her. And an old

man said politely, 'Could you move
your leg, sonny, it's forcing me into the
road.'

But Nick couldn't move it because
Mum had tied it firmly to an old broom
handle with two woolly football scarves.

It looked ridiculous.

'Please,' he prayed, as they approached the school bus stop, 'please let the bus have gone . . . '

But it had just drawn up at the kerb and everyone he knew was piling on. 'Look at Nick Butler!' someone shouted, and they all did, pointing and jabbing at him through the back window like a cart-load of monkeys.

'Out Patients' was a large room on the ground floor of the hospital and it was crowded with people all waiting to see the doctor. Mum explained about Nick's pain and two nurses came up with a special wheel chair. It had a little platform fixed to the front so that he could sit with his legs sticking out.

'What about the broom handle?' he whispered. It looked so stupid.

'Oh, don't worry about that, dear,'

they said. 'Just relax. Doctor'll be along very soon, he'll sort you out.'

But Nick didn't feel like relaxing. 'Soon' was going to be hours, from the look of this queue, and what did 'sorting him out' mean? He was starting to feel rather nervous.

Nobody emerged from the brown door labelled DOCTOR for at least ten minutes, then a cheery old lady hobbled out, on two sticks. Ellie had been busy flinging toys round the room and she was dreadfully smelly now. People were beginning to back away. Then a nurse with a label that said SISTER SPINDLER came bustling up. 'I think we'll take you next,' she said, wrinkling her nose. 'Come along.' And she ticked Nick's name off on a list.

'Good old Ellie,' he thought, 'if it wasn't for her we'd still be at the end of that queue.'

Soon they were all following Sister Spindler along endless shiny corridors. First he had a lot of X-rays, then he was weighed and measured. Then someone looked in his ears and down his throat and asked him if he liked football and had he ever had the pain before. Sister

Spindler wrote all the answers down and stuffed them into an envelope. He was obviously a very important case *indeed*.

But when he was wheeled in to see Professor Vrodsky, the special 'bone doctor', he had a bit of a let-down. It seemed that his pain wasn't special at all, that millions of people had them, all the time.

The professor had a beard and a pointy kind of head, and he strode up and down looking at Nick's X-ray photos. What he saw was

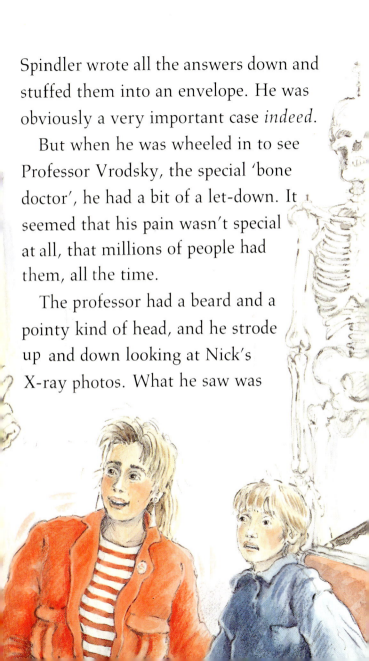

making him very excited.

'You see ziss, Meezus Butler . . . and ziss . . . Ziss iss a perfect example, a vonderful example, off *ZEE HIP FLU*.'

'I beg your pardon?' Mum said politely. 'How can you get flu in your leg?'

Nick didn't understand either. 'Flu' was about sore throats and sneezes, not about sudden awful pains in your leg, whenever you tried to stand up.

'Here iss zee joint off zee right hip,' said Dr Vrodsky. 'Look very carefully, please. You will see a nasty leetle black patch. Zat iss zee fluid, zee water. The hip hass caught a leetle cold. When zee boy stand up, *pouf*! He gets pain. Nobody know why or how ziss happen. It just *happen*.'

'Er, I see,' Mum said. 'So what's the cure for this, er, "flu", Doctor?'

Nick was already thinking about going home. He would probably be given a few pills and be told to rest. No Miss Huggett for ages. *Great*.

'From here, you go straight to zee Hilton. Iss zee best place, zee only place, for ziss boy.'

Nick perked up even more. The Hilton was the poshest place in town. 'The Hilton *Hotel*?' he whispered.

'Well, of *course* not, Nick,' Mum said. 'Dr Vrodsky means the Hilton *Hospital*.'

'Iss correct. Zee Hilton Bone Hospital. Iss fantastic. Hass all that iss needed to cure bad legs. Ziss boy he stay in bed, his leg in zee air. He not move. *Pouf*! All iss well, he hop about. I make ziss arrangement now.' And he picked up a telephone.

'His leg in the *air*?' What on earth did

that mean? But there was no time to ask
questions. 'Come along, everyone,'
trilled Sister Spindler. 'There's an
ambulance ready and waiting.'

Soon they were rolling quietly
through town in the back of a sleek
white van. No alarm bells rang to
scatter the traffic and they stopped at all
the red lights. Nick felt a bit cheated,
and perfectly well. He wasn't at all sure

he wanted a week in this 'Hilton', and when he saw it he was *quite* sure. The other hospital had been big, new and shiny. The Hilton Bone Hospital was just a few decrepit huts arranged round a patch of scruffy grass. It looked a bit like their school lavatories.

The rear doors were opened and a ramp let down, so he could be rolled off in his special chair. Mum went first,

with Ellie and the broom handle.

Out came a nurse to meet them. Her badge said SISTER TROTMAN. 'I'm looking after you,' she told Nick. 'You'll have a good time in Ward Nine, there's a friend of yours in it. He fell off his bicycle and broke his leg.'

Nick felt slightly more cheerful when he heard that. A whole week in this hut place with nothing whatever to do didn't appeal to him at all. But if there was a *friend* to talk to . . . Who could it be?

He found out when they wheeled him into the ward. You couldn't exactly miss the great shock of carrot-coloured hair, the bulgy blue eye-balls, the freckles; and there was no mistaking the glass-shattering voice.

'Hi, Nick,' it yelled across the room. On bedside lockers, water-jugs tinkled faintly.

'Oh, *no*,' he thought, closing his eyes, 'what's *he* doing here?' It was Marcus Hogg-Robinson from their class: Marcus, the terror of the back row, who'd once shoved a cheese-and-pickle sandwich down the back of Nick's trousers.

'Mum,' he said, as the nurses stopped by an empty bed and got ready to lift him out of the chair, 'Mum, why can't I get better at home?'

The bed was high and wide, with all sorts of interesting contraptions attached to it, and a view of the scruffy grass plot through the window behind. *But it was right next to Marcus Hogg-Robinson's.*

Chapter 2

MARCUS'S LEFT LEG looked enormous. It was covered in thick white plaster from top to bottom. All you could see were five pink toes wiggling about at the end, like sausages waiting for the frying pan. He was obviously dying to have a chat with Nick.

'It was a *terrible* break,' he said enthusiastically. 'It was a *comminuted compound femoral fracture*. But Professor Vrodsky says I'm doing really well. I'm getting crutches tomorrow. What's up with you, then?'

'Hip flu,' replied Nick, with a touch of pride.

'Oh, is that all?' Marcus said crushingly. 'Listen, what do you think of my plaster?'

Nick glanced across at it as Sister Trotman put screens round his bed and Mum helped him into the bed.

It was covered with writing: 'Marcus Was Here', 'More Jelly for Marcus', and 'Marcus Rules OK'. He was just a big show-off.

'It's OK,' he said coolly, as the screens went up, and he pretended to be going to sleep. But when they were removed he was quite anxious that Marcus should have a good look at him. His right leg was sticking straight up in the air now, and he'd got great weights fixed to the end of a special pulley thing.

'I'm on traction,' he said airily ('traction' was what Sister Trotman had called it, as they'd hoisted his leg towards the ceiling). 'It's just to make sure I don't move my leg, till the flu's gone away.'

'Very nice . . . yes . . . great . . . ' Marcus muttered, pointedly opening a book. But Nick could see he was jealous. Loads of people in the ward had plasters, but nobody else had a leg in the air.

He didn't need to worry about having to talk to Marcus, the nurses kept everyone far too busy. First there were milky drinks, then there was tidying lockers and straightening sheets. Then there was lunch on a tray, then it was 'naps'. Even if you didn't feel like going to sleep you had to keep quiet. Marcus was wide awake, though, and busy with an advanced Lego model of a North Sea oil rig. He was brilliant at making things. He wanted to be an inventor.

Nick had nothing to do. Mum couldn't come back till after tea so he had nothing to read, nothing to draw on and nothing interesting to eat. Idly he looked out of the window, across the square of scruffy grass. Over the rooftops he could see flags fluttering on top of the travelling circus tents. It was only in town for a week and Mum had promised to take him. They wouldn't be going now, though.

The hospital grounds were empty apart from one small figure, a fat little man who, as Nick watched, shambled slowly towards the hut. Nick half shut his eyes and kept very still, but all the time he was peeping. The man was right up at the window now, staring in. He had a jolly face, round and red as if it had been boiled, and a shaggy mass of grisly grey hair straggling down from underneath his smart bowler hat. It didn't really match the rest of his outfit, old baggy trousers and a long trailing raincoat held together with safety pins.

He was now so close his breath had turned the glass all foggy. Nick gave a little wave and the old man waved back. Then he started tapping on the window.

Nick stretched forwards and opened it. 'Hello,' he whispered, rather nervous. All the hair made the old man a bit ferocious-looking, but the round

red face was kind. 'Hello, mate,' he whispered, and he touched his bowler hat politely. 'So, what have you been doing to yourself then?' He was staring with interest at the weights and the pulley.

'Oh, nothing, I've got flu in my leg,

that's all. Having it up in the air'll get it better, Dr Vrodsky says. It's dead boring though, just lying here, and the nurses make such a *fuss* . . . '

'Yeah, I know,' said the little man, 'fuss, fuss, *fuss* . . . they fuss about me too, mate. They don't like me going through the dustbins. But, as I've told them, a man's got to live and you get some really good stuff thrown out with the rubbish. Take this coat, for example . . . ' and he stroked his lapel.

'Er, it's lovely,' Nick said, 'really great.' He could tell that the funny old man was proud of it.

'What d'you think of the grub then?'

'Well, so far I've only had lunch. It was cold, and the potatoes were lumpy.'

'Don't tell me, mate. Terrible food here. Now old Nurse Plackett's the one to get friendly with, she always saves

me something tasty. Met Nurse
Plackett, have you?'

Nick was just opening his mouth to
reply when Sister Trotman came
buzzing up. 'Shoo!' she hissed, flapping
her arms at the jolly red face. Instantly
the old man dropped away from the
window and scurried off over the grass.

'Who was that?' Nick said, settling
down obediently in his bed as she puffed
up his pillows and tidied his sheets (they
were mad on tidying, in Ward Nine).

'Oh, it's only Arthur. He's a bit of a
nuisance.'

'Is he, er, a tramp?' That raincoat he
was so proud of was in ribbons, though
the bowler hat was rather fine.

'Sort of. He lives in a hostel down the
road, with some other old men. But he's
always hanging round here, I'm afraid.
He likes his food, does Arthur. Now

then, have a nice little snooze and don't worry your head about him.'

Nick shut his eyes. He wasn't worrying, in fact he'd thought Arthur looked good fun. He'd rather be talking to him than have to listen to Marcus boring on about his oil rig. Though he must have reached a difficult part because he'd dozed off and was making the most awful snoring noises. How could you get any sleep with that row?

After 'naps' the visitors came. Everyone had somebody except Nick. He felt out of it. Mum couldn't come till much later and Dad not at all: he was on his ship, somewhere in mid Atlantic. Then he saw Grandad marching up between the beds, his face split in two by a wide grin. 'Hello, there, feller-me-lad. What have you been up to, then?'

'Nothing. Only, I've got this pain.

It's the flu, Professor Vrodsky says.'

Grandad inspected the weights-and-pulley arrangement. 'Those are whopping great weights,' he said, 'you'd better be careful. You don't want one falling on your toe.'

'No chance,' Nick said gloomily. 'I've got to stay in this bed for a whole week. I'm bored.'

But Grandad had brought him a 'lucky bag'. Diving in, he produced: six comics, a drawing book and pencils, a bunch of bananas, a tub of peanuts and a telescope. Nick put it to his eye and focused on Marcus's toes. Through the glass they looked huge, mega-sausages now.

'It's just to keep you out of mischief,' said Grandad. He'd been in the Navy too, like Dad. He knew how much Nick liked that old brass telescope.

'*Thanks*, Grandad,' and they had a big hug.

When visiting time was over Nick ate one of his bananas and spied on everyone with the telescope. He could see every single freckle on Marcus's nose now, and the whiskers of Lucy Bailey's blue rabbit, on the opposite bed, and the little gold rings in Sister Trotman's ears. Through his window he could see the circus flags and old Arthur rummaging about in a plastic sack. Nick tried waving but the old man didn't notice. If Sister Trotman saw him she'd probably come and shoo him away again.

He felt lonely. Everyone else seemed to have their own special friend and Marcus was too busy with his oil rig to do any talking. Glumly he opened one of his comics. He'd only been here a few hours and the time was crawling. He couldn't even watch television with the other children, it was too far away.

By bedtime he was feeling a bit more cheerful. Mum had been with Ellie, and the nurses had made a big fuss of her. While they'd fussed Mum had loaded his locker with goodies: biscuits, more bananas, and a big box of sweets from the Mackenzies next door. 'You've got

enough to feed an army now,' she said. 'Don't eat too many snacks, you'll get tummy ache. If I were you I'd – Good Heavens!' and she jerked up, from down by the bed.

'What's up?'

'Well, there was someone looking in, an old man . . . '

'Oh, that's Arthur.'

'And who's Arthur? The gardener?'

NO PARKING

He was shambling away now, towards the hospital gates.

'Er, sort of.'

'Funny time to be doing the garden,' said Mum.

When everyone had gone home Nick settled down for a night's sleep. It took ages because his right leg felt so peculiar, sticking straight up, but at last he was drifting nicely, and having funny mixed-up dreams about Noah's Flood. Dad and Sister Trotman were rowing up and down Ward Nine in a rubber dinghy.

When he woke up it was still dark. By the bed his yellow alarm said 11.30. Down at the end of the room, old Nurse Plackett, who was on Night Duty, was sitting in front of the television. He blinked and looked around, wondering what had woken him up. Then he saw something moving about on the other side of the ward, something little and dark. 'Hey!' he yelled, grabbing his telescope.

In the opposite bed, little Lucy Bailey started to cry. She said she'd lost her blue rabbit and that a horrible noise had woken her up. 'Nurse!' she screeched, '*Nurse*! I've lost Timmy down the bed. I was dreaming and . . . and . . . *something horrid touched my face*!'

Nurse Plackett came hobbling up and found Timmy under the pillow, straightened her sheets and gave her a cuddle. 'Just a nasty dream, duckie,' she clucked. 'Settle down, nightie night.' Then she saw Nick, sitting bolt upright with his telescope. 'You all right, dear?' she said. 'Can I get you anything?'

'No, no, it's OK, thanks . . . '

'Well, toodle pip, then,' and she toddled back to the late night movie.

The minute she'd gone Nick whipped his telescope out from under the bedclothes and trained it on that funny

dark shape he'd seen, by Lucy's bed. But
it had gone. He stared down the big
brass tube for ages but all he could see
were huddled sleeping shapes, and
curtains blowing gently in the breeze
from an open window.

Chapter 3

IN THE MORNING a blood-curdling yell
from Marcus made everybody jump out
of their skins. 'My bananas!' he
bellowed. 'They've gone! Every single
one of them! Come on, who's pinched
them?'

'Don't look at *me*,' Nick said rather
huffily. 'How could I reach them, stuck
in this bed? Anyhow, I've got bananas
of my own.'

But when he looked in his fruit bowl
they'd vanished.

After that everyone started checking
their lockers and there were complaints
from all over the ward. 'My bananas

have gone too!' someone yelled. 'And my chocolates!' another shouted. 'All my biscuits have been eaten, it's not *fair* . . . ' snivelled a third. The cries came from all sides.

'Now come *along*, everybody,' Mrs Saltmarsh the hospital teacher said briskly, as she walked between the beds doling out paper and pencils. 'All this fuss about food disappearing has got to stop. I'm sure nobody's been eating your things. Settle down now, it's school time.'

School? Nick just couldn't believe it. He'd planned to have a week off while his flu went away, and here was Miss Saltmarsh with two pages of sums from Miss Huggett. 'Special Delivery'. *Yuk.*

Marcus saw him puzzling over them, came straight over on his new crutches and showed him exactly what to do. He

was brilliant, miles better than
Miss Huggett. Could this really be
Marcus Hogg-Robinson, the terror of
the back row? He was being quite
human.

'Thanks, Marcus,' said Nick.

'That's OK. Easy-Peasy, when you
know how. Now listen, what I really
came to say was, *what about all this
food that's disappearing?*'

'What about it? I suppose it's someone in the ward, I mean, someone who gets hungry in the middle of the night.'

'Ne'er,' Marcus said scornfully. 'Look at this.' From his pyjama pocket he took a piece of newspaper cut out from something called *The Spotlight*. 'My mum brought it for me,' he said. 'She knows I'm mad on animals.'

Nick stretched out his hand but Marcus kept the cutting tantalizingly at arm's length. 'What's dark and hairy and likes bananas?' he said. 'And peanuts?'

Nick shrugged.

'Lulu, of course.'

'*Lulu?*'

Marcus unfolded the news cutting. 'LULU DOES A BUNK' read the headline. She was a chimpanzee from the travelling circus and she'd disappeared from her cage. There was a big photo of her wearing a bowler hat and pouring herself a cup of tea.

Nick's mouth dropped open. 'I don't *believe* it,' he whispered. 'Last night, over by Lucy's bed, I saw something moving about.'

'What was it like? Was it wearing a bowler hat?'

'Dunno. I only saw it for a second.'

'Was it dark and hairy?'

Nick hesitated. 'Well, it *could* have been . . . '

'That's it, then,' Marcus said decisively. 'We're after Lulu. What else would creep round here at night stealing other people's bananas?'

Nick didn't answer. It just seemed too ridiculous. But the fruit *had* been stolen, *and* the biscuits, *and* the sweets. And Lulu had definitely disappeared from the circus. When Mum came he was dying to ask her if there was any news on the missing chimp but he'd promised that he'd keep quiet. Marcus Hogg-Robinson had a PLAN.

Mrs Butler hadn't had any lunch. Ellie had been playing up all morning and there'd been no time. So she

decided to have a few of Grandad's
peanuts. 'Good *grief*,' she said, getting
the tub out of Nick's locker. 'You've
been stuffing yourself, haven't you?
Half of these have gone. You're going to
be ill, my lad.'

'But *Mum*,' he protested, 'I'd not
even *opened* them.'

Sister Trotman, whizzing past,

flashed him a brilliant smile. 'Oh, I expect it's that monkey, dear,' she said, 'the one who's escaped from the zoo and eaten all the fruit and chocolates,' and she exchanged a knowing wink with Mum.

Before she went home Mrs Butler delivered a lecture about not being greedy and getting a stomach ache.

'You're better off with fruit,' she said, 'if you want a snack. It's a good job I brought some more bananas. I see you've polished those off, too.'

'Thanks,' said Nick meekly, lying back in bed as she arranged them in the fruit bowl. It was no earthly use telling her or the nurses about the chimp in the night. They obviously thought the children had eaten all the food themselves.

After tea he had a serious talk with Marcus and explained about the missing peanuts.

'*Right*,' announced Marcus in a very important kind of voice. 'Peanuts equals Lulu. Chimps'll eat anything, but they *adore* peanuts. Nobody in this ward could have eaten as many as that. They'd burst. Tonight, my friend, we've just got to stay awake . . . ' and he got on to his crutches and they huddled down out of sight, by Nick's locker. The plan was to keep watch that night, and see Lulu doing her rounds. Nick would set his alarm for 11.30, just in case they dozed off. Old Nurse Plackett was on Night Duty again. Fortunately for them, she was a little bit deaf.

As a treat she let the older ones watch a film on television before going to sleep. Nick's bed was pulled away from the wall so that he could watch, too.

It was a great movie, an old 'Tarzan and Jane', with plenty of chimps in it, gobbling bananas. It was almost as if Nurse Plackett knew about their little plan. But it went on so long that both boys were yawning well before the end. Nick hardly noticed when she wheeled him back and helpfully switched off his alarm clock. When 11.30 came they were both sound asleep.

In the morning there were more wails and moans. All the remaining bananas had vanished, along with some fudge and Lucy's chocolate panda from her Auntie Lil. This time, Sister Trotman went round with a clip-board. She was particularly interested in people who could walk about, people like Marcus Hogg-Robinson . . .

When she'd gone he shook his fist at her. 'She thinks it's *me*,' he told Nick, through gritted teeth, 'I'm *positive* she thinks it's me.'

'Yes, but we know who it is, don't we?' Nick replied smugly, 'and we went and fell asleep, didn't we? The thing is, to catch Lulu *in the act*.'

'OK,' Marcus said. 'It's time to put

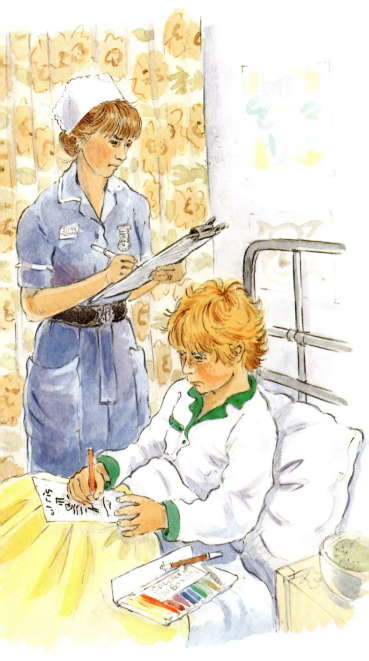

my second plan into action, I mean my *big* plan.'

They whispered together for ages, working things out, and during 'naps' Nick wrote a list of all the things they were going to need, sticky tape, string, some very strong wire and a penknife. He knew it was no good asking his Mum, she'd never bring such interesting things into a hospital. But Grandad would understand. So Nick borrowed the 'travelling phone', plugged it in by the bed, and rang him up. '*Please*, Grandad,' he pleaded. 'Only, Marcus has invented this brilliant monkey trap. It's just a joke,' he added hastily, 'but we'd like to see if it'd work.'

'All right, young feller-me-lad.' Grandad was a bit of an inventor himself, and the monkey trap idea obviously tickled him. 'I'll pop the stuff in some time today,' he said. 'My word, you lads'll be catching that Lulu next. She's still around, you know . . . ' And he rang off, with a chuckle.

'He doesn't believe we're serious,' Nick said, as he put the phone down.

'But will he bring the stuff?'

'Oh yes, Grandad never lets me down.'

And he didn't. He called in during evening visiting with what he described as 'a few biscuits for my starving grandson'. But inside the big tin he'd brought were all the things they needed: sticky tape, penknife, wire, and a piece of thick string coiled round like a snake. Grandad had been in the Navy like Dad. He was always neat and ship-shape. The one thing Nick had forgotten to ask for was a long piece of wood, but

they were in luck there. Mum had forgotten to take her broom handle home and it'd been tidied away under his bed by Sister Trotman.

While Nick was checking the contents of the biscuit tin, Marcus was busy drawing complicated diagrams. When nobody was looking he crept out of bed and examined Nick's weights-and-pulley contraption very carefully. It was all made up of metal tubes, of chains and springs. In the middle was a thick piece of brown cord. It looked very strong to Marcus.

He clambered back into bed, muttering to himself. 'Hmm . . . if that pivots there, and we have a pulley here . . . then we'd need a counterbalance . . . I just hope it's a strong penknife!'

That evening, during telly time,

when the ward was dim, Marcus stayed in bed and put his great invention together. Then he went on his rounds. Nick's job was to receive the food and keep it out of sight. It was rather awful, watching Marcus hopping round the ward on his crutches, slipping things from people's lockers down inside his dressing gown. But they'd get everything back tomorrow, if the plan worked.

What if it *didn't* work, though? Nick refused to think about that, and he refused to look at Marcus's invention, too. Now it had been put together it looked quite terrifying. If only Marcus could become an inventor *now*. Miss Huggett would have no more trouble with him, stuffing his packed lunch down people's trousers.

The last part of the plan couldn't be

carried out until Nurse Plackett had done her final rounds for the night. Then, when she was in the nurses' pantry, boiling a kettle, Marcus pulled his invention out from behind a curtain and fixed it into position. Meanwhile, Nick arranged all the food at the bottom of his bed: bananas, biscuits, crisps, and the last of Grandad's peanuts. Then he waited, his heart in his mouth. What if Lulu got angry, and bit somebody? And what would they *do* with her, while Sister Trotman phoned the circus?

He lay there for ages, dozing and worrying, worrying and dozing, but in no time at all his clock was saying 11.30 in glaring white figures. And something was moving about at the other end of the ward, something little and black and shaggy with a humped round head. It was Lulu. She wouldn't be parted from

that bowler hat. It had said so in the paper.

It didn't take long for her to reach Nick's bed. She was after food, and the other fruit-bowls and lockers had been emptied of their goodies by Marcus. But here, spread out under the leg, was a wonderful midnight feast. It was just the thing for a hungry chimpanzee. The little black figure stopped, crunched a

few biscuits, then hovered over the tub of peanuts. Marcus, wide awake and sitting up, started a regular sawing motion . . .

CRASH! The whole of Ward Nine was awake and lights were coming on everywhere. Nurses Trotman and Plackett were rushing down between the beds. '*Help*!' squeaked the chimp half-way through a banana. Its bowler hat

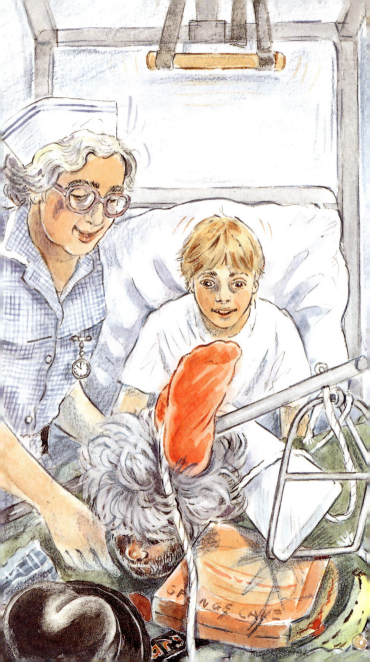

had been rammed down on to its nose and it was wriggling under a tangle of bed-clothes, pulleys and chains. Nick's leg was no longer up in the air, it was level and flat and normal, and it had dented the bowler hat.

'Gotcha!' yelled Marcus, letting go of the broom handle.

'Arthur?' enquired Nurse Plackett anxiously, peeping under Nick's blankets. 'Arthur, are you all right?'

'*Come out of there!*' thundered Sister Trotman.

By the end of the week Lulu was back at the circus (they'd found her eating popcorn in the cinema). And Nick was back home. When he walked about there was no pain at all, just a wobbly, dreamy feeling in the region of his right leg. He'd not used it for such a long time.

Marcus went home too. He was brilliant on his crutches now and he'd developed rippling biceps. He took his broom-handle invention with him. Mrs Butler had bought a new brush.

There was talk of getting the police in, to deal with Arthur, but in the end he was let off with a rocketing from Sister Trotman. He told her that he got awful hunger pains during the night, and that he'd not been able to resist all the goodies in the children's lockers, especially Nick's peanuts. The food in his hostel was even worse than the hospital's. Nurse Plackett felt so sorry that she made him a great big cake.

The day before Nick went back to school he saw him sitting on a bench at the bottom of their street. His jolly red face didn't look quite so jolly as before; he looked thinner, too, and there were even more safety pins holding his coat together. Nick felt a bit sorry for him. Who cared about a few bananas and nuts anyhow? They'd had a lot of fun with their chimpanzee trap.

Grandad had brought another big tub of peanuts to say 'Welcome Home'. He wouldn't mind if they were shared out amongst friends. Nick ran upstairs and came down with them under his arm. Then he made his way down the street.